Anna Wilson lives Northamptonshire with he children and two black cats called Ink and Jet. She has written two picture books and plans many more books in the

Nina
Fairy Ballerina
series.

Nicola Slater lives in the north of England with Dave the cat. Her work can be seen on books and tablecloths around the globe.

Look out for the other books in the

Nina Fairy Ballerina

series

New Girl

Daisy Shoes

Best Friends

Coming soon

Flying Colours

Double Trouble

Party Magic

Dream Treat

Compiled by Anna Wilson

Princess Stories

Fairy Stories

Nina
Fairy Ballerina

Show Time

Anna Wilson

Illustrated by Nicola Slater

MACMILLAN CHILDREN'S BOOKS

For all the children and teachers at
Stamford Junior School

First published 2006 by Macmillan Children's Books
a division of Macmillan Publishers Limited
20 New Wharf Road, London N1 9RR
Basingstoke and Oxford
www.panmacmillan.com

Associated companies throughout the world

ISBN-13: 978-0-330-43988-6
ISBN-10: 0-330-43988-X

Text copyright © Anna Wilson 2006
Illustrations copyright © Nicola Slater 2006

The right of Anna Wilson and Nicola Slater to be identified as the author
and illustrator of this book has been asserted by them in accordance
with the Copyright, Designs and Patents Act 1988.

1 3 5 7 9 8 6 4 2

A CIP catalogue record for this book is available from
the British Library.

Typeset by Nigel Hazle
Printed and bound in Great Britain by Mackays of Chatham plc, Kent

Chapter One

"Bella, you can't bring any more bags in here!" Nina protested.

"Why not?" Bella answered grumpily.

"If I'm going to stay at the Academy, I'll need more than an overnight bag."

Bella Glove was joining the Royal Academy of Fairy Ballet. It was obvious to everyone that she didn't belong at the Jazz School, where she'd been before. Her mother, Foxy Glove, was a famous jazz dancer and she'd assumed that her daughter would follow in her footsteps. But, like Nina, Bella was a born to be a ballerina.

There was, however, a slight problem: Bella had been sharing Nina and Peri's room on Charlock corridor and space was getting very tight.

"You had a lot more than an overnight bag in the first place, Bella!" Peri said.

"Yeah, you're right," Bella admitted grudgingly. She looked at the mountain of luggage and sighed. "Hey, I guess you wouldn't let me say a little spell to help me with this lot, Nina?"

Nina gasped. "Bella, how could you!

After all the trouble your spells have already got you into. And don't forget, Queen Camellia has invited us to the palace to put on a show. Madame Dupré will never let us go if you—"

"OK! Keep your wings on!" Bella laughed. "Let's go and ask Madame Dupré what we should do."

The headmistress's office was a cosy little room. The walls were lined with shelves crammed with ballet books.

Madame Dupré was fluttering to and fro above her beechnut desk, dictating a letter to her secretary, Miss Meadowsweet.

"Madame, we've got a problem!" Peri said as she burst into the room.

Miss Meadowsweet leaped up and dropped her lily pad and pen in shock. "Really, Periwinkle," she cried. "You know that you should knock before interrupting the headmistress."

"It's all right," said Madame Dupré
kindly. "I can see that Periwinkle's
enthusiasm has run away with her again.
However, Periwinkle, please do try to
remember your manners in future."

Peri's face went as red as her hair.
"Yes, Madame," she said quietly.

"You'd better come in," the
headmistress suggested.
"You obviously have
something of great
importance to
tell me."

The three
fairy friends shuffled
into the office.
Madame Dupré
motioned to them
to sit down on
three small
toadstools. "Go on,
Periwinkle," she said.
"I'm listening."

"The thing is, Madame, now that Bella's staying on at the Academy, it's a bit of a tight squeeze in our room. She has been sleeping on the pull-out guest bed, so there hasn't been much floor space. And now that all her luggage has been brought over from the Jazz School there's not enough room to swing a gnat . . ." Peri stopped and took a deep breath. "So we were wondering if you could think of a solution. Please," she added.

"I see," said the headmistress. "You're absolutely right, Periwinkle. There is no way that Bella can continue to live like this."

Nina and Peri gasped. Were the three fairy friends going to be separated?

"Don't worry," Madame Dupré laughed. "No one's going to split up the Dream Team!" Just then the bluebell rang to call the fairy ballerinas to their classes. "Fly along now, fairies, and just leave this little problem to me."

Chapter Two

ina, Peri and Bella were the last to arrive in the studio.

"Well, if it isn't the Terrible Trio!" said their teacher, Miss Tremula. "Come along now — you're just in time for the warm-up."

Mrs Wisteria began to play a dreamy piece of music on the piano, and the fairy ballerinas lined up at the barre.

"Stretch your arms above your heads, fairies," Miss Tremula said. "Imagine you are a beautiful tulip, unfurling in the morning sun."

The ballerinas
moved gracefully
and carefully. All
except Peri, that
is. She could not
concentrate on her ballet
positions. She was too worried
about what would happen to
Bella. I can't imagine us not
being together, Peri thought.
"Periwinkle, please pay

attention – and straighten out your tights,
will you dear?" Miss Tremula admonished.
"You look more like a tumbleweed than a
tulip."

Peri hoisted up her tights and tried
hard to copy her teacher's moves for the
rest of the warm-up.

"Now, let's return to the ballet we
will be performing for Queen Camellia,"
said Miss Tremula. "Madame Dupré was
very impressed with your interpretation of
the ballet *Petrushka*, especially as you are
still only in your first year. It has been
agreed that you, Nina, will play the part
of the Ballerina – a fitting part for our
scholarship fairy."

Yes! thought Nina. I'll be able to
dance in my daisy shoes at last! "Bella,
you will be the Moor," Miss Tremula
continued, "and Periwinkle, you have the
title role – that of Petrushka the clown.
At least it won't matter if your tights are
a little wrinkled when you dance *that*

part!" Miss Tremula teased gently.

"What about the rest of us, miss?" asked Nyssa Bean, another of Nina's friends.

"Don't worry, Nyssa," Miss Tremula reassured her. "There are plenty of exciting roles in this ballet. There is the cruel Showman, for example. He owns the puppets and gets them to dance by playing his flute."

"Sounds like a role for Angelica Nightshade," whispered Peri. Nina giggled. Angelica was an older fairy who was very big-headed and had been unkind to Nina when she had first joined the Academy.

Miss Tremula carried on telling

the class about the other parts. There was a Russian dancer, an organ-grinder – even a Dancing Bear!

"So you see, no one will be left out," explained their teacher.

Just then Miss Meadowsweet hurried into the studio.

"I am sorry to disturb you, Miss Tremula," she said a little breathlessly, "but I have some important news for Nina, Periwinkle and Bella."

"What is it, Miss M?" asked Nina nervously.

"The problem of your room-share has been solved for the moment. Her Royal Fairyness Queen Camellia, has requested your presence this very morning!" Miss Meadowsweet said, beaming. "One of her carriages is waiting outside now!"

The fairy friends gasped. A royal carriage – just like Cinderella! thought Nina.

Chapter Three

Nina, Peri and Bella flitted out of the Academy's glittering gold gates. There, waiting for them, was a shimmering silver carriage drawn by four dazzling dragonflies. It certainly was a carriage fit for a fairy queen! A neatly dressed coachman was there to greet them, accompanied by two smart footmen. They wore long lilac frock coats and huge lilac powdered wigs. Their wings were lilac too.

"Would modom care to step this way?" the coachman asked haughtily, and he held open the carriage door.

"Who's modom?" Peri asked, puzzled.

"Duh, he means you!" Bella whispered.

The three fairies dissolved into fits of giggles.

"Her Majesty is expecting you," the coachman said huffily. "She is not accustomed to being kept waiting."

The three fairies stifled their laughter, climbed into the carriage and sat down. Their suitcases had already been packed for them and were under the seats.

"Fasten your seat belts," one of the footmen commanded.

"Seat belts?" queried Nina. "Why do we need s—"

WHOOOSH! Nina didn't have time

to finish her question. The carriage surged up into the air, and the fairies were thrown back into their silken seats.

"Wow!" said Bella when she'd recovered from the shock. "I guess that's what happens when you put four dragonflies together."

The carriage whizzed down the drive and was soon hurtling deep into the surrounding woodland. Once she'd got used to the speed, Peri pressed her face up against the window to have a look out. As she did so, she could have sworn that a cheeky little face appeared and stuck its tongue out at her. Peri blinked – the face had gone. She shivered.

"A bit creepy, isn't it?" she said nervously. "I've never liked dark woods. You don't know what might be lurking around the corner." She didn't want to tell her friends what she thought she had seen, in case they laughed at her.

"Don't worry, Peri," Bella reassured

her. "We must be pretty safe in this thing." She knocked on the wall of the carriage to show Peri how tough it was.

Immediately, one of the footmen appeared at the window, holding a firefly as a torch.

"Do you require assistance?" he asked.

The three friends hid their laughter behind their hands. The footman was hovering so quickly that his wig was slowly slipping over his eyes.

"No assistance required," Bella just managed to squeak out.

"Well, please do not knock then," the footman said sniffily. "We are travelling at high speed as you can see, and any unnecessary disruptions will not be tolerated. I will inform you of our arrival in due course."

With that, the footman disappeared from the window. The three friends couldn't control their laughter any longer.

"What's he like!" Peri

hooted, her earlier fear now forgotten. "I hope they're not all like that at the palace. I'll never be able to concentrate on the show!"

Nina giggled. "I've a feeling Queen Camellia is going to prove to be quite a character too," she said. "I can't wait to meet her!"

Chapter Four

SCREECH! The carriage halted abruptly.

The footman reappeared and, discreetly readjusting his wonky wig, announced, "Welcome to the Royal Palace."

Nina, Peri and Bella alighted from the carriage and looked up . . . and up!

The palace was immense. It had so many windows – not to mention turrets, towers and spires – that it made the fairies feel quite dizzy. At first glance, the walls seemed to be painted white, but

*•** 18 *•*•*

when the friends moved nearer they
noticed a shimmering, rainbow haze on
the surface.

The footman led the way through
glimmering gates. They made the ones at
the Academy look positively puny! On
arriving at some large mahogany doors,
he rapped on the wood with his wand
and called out:

Queen Camellia's guests are here.
They've come at her request.
They are three ballerinas
(Giggly and poorly dressed).
Please let them in and give them tea —
They are to have the best —
Then bring them smartly back to me
And I will do the rest.

"Poorly dressed!" Bella huffed. "He's the
one with the candyfloss on his head!"

"Shh!" Peri whispered.

She was sure she heard someone

behind them giggle quietly. But when she turned round, no one was there. She was about to ask her friends if they'd heard anything when – DING! – three tiny fairies appeared and called out to the friends to follow them.

The ballerinas were taken straight to a cosy drawing room with a roaring fire. In front of the fire, tea had been laid out for them.

"Yummy! Hot chocolate with sprinkles – my favourite!" Peri cried, launching herself at the food.

"Caraway-seed cake too!" Nina said, laughing. "What a treat!"

"Mffchffsh!" Bella agreed, her cheeks bulging.

Suddenly Peri's hot chocolate leaped out of her mug in an arc and landed down the front of her crossover cardigan.

"Argh!" she screamed. She tried in vain to brush it off, but only succeeded in making matters worse. There's that

giggle again,
Peri thought,
looking round
quickly. But
again, no one
was there.

"What are
you doing?" Nina
cried. "Look at the
state of you! Quick, take
your cardy off – I
think I hear
someone
coming."

"But I didn't do it
– didn't you see?" Peri
protested. But Bella
and Nina didn't
seem to know what
Peri was talking about and hurriedly
helped her to remove the offending
garment.

"Trust you to be clumsy," Bella

muttered, stuffing the cardigan down the back of the sofa.

"Shh!" Nina urged. "Don't start arguing now. We have to be on our best behaviour, remember?"

The footman reappeared and asked the friends to follow him to the Ballroom. The fairies were astonished. It was three times the size of the Grand Hall at the Academy, and far more sumptuous. The ceiling was painted with dancing fairies and stars, and the round windows were hung with gossamer curtains. The floor was highly polished marble. I hope I don't slip over, thought Nina nervously.

Queen Camellia sat on a jewel-encrusted throne, high on a glittering plinth. She was the most beautiful fairy Nina had ever seen. She had silky hair that was so blonde it was almost white. It was held back softly from her delicate face with hundreds of tiny diamond pins.

She wore a diamond crown
too. Her gown shone so
brightly it looked as
though it were
made of stars.

"Your
Majesty," said
the footman,
bowing low,
"Nina Dewdrop,
Periwinkle
Moonshine and Bella
Glove."

"Thank you,
Teasel," the queen
said. Her voice was
like a silver bell that
rang out across the
room. "That will be
all." And she
dismissed him with a
wave of her wand.

The fairies curtseyed just as

Miss Tremula had taught them, and bowed their heads low.

Please don't let there be any hot-chocolate stains on my leotard, Peri prayed silently.

"Up you get now, fairies!" said the queen. "We've got work to do."

Chapter Five

Nina and her friends quickly warmed to Queen Camellia. She's so easy to talk to! thought Nina.

"I am so pleased that you are here," the queen was saying. "My daughter, Princess Coriander, is very keen on ballet. She can't wait to see the show. Don't worry though," the queen added hastily. "I'm not letting her in on the preparations. She's far too young and she would only get in the way."

"We are very pleased to be here too," Nina said politely. "This is the first time

we've done a real show — not to mention
a royal one." Nina went on to explain
the fairies' roles in the ballet. "I'm going
to be the Ballerina; Bella's going to be
the Moor who I fall in love with—"

"She doesn't *really* fall in love with
me," Bella butted in hastily.

Nina giggled. "Of course not, silly!
And Peri, well, she's got the best role of
all — she is going to be Petrushka the
clown." Nina grinned at Peri.

"Lovely!" the queen said kindly. "And
you must be full of ideas for the scenery.
Will you help me decorate this stage for
the ballet?"

"That would be wonderful, Your
Royal Fairyness!" Peri cried, bursting like
a bubble with excitement.

The queen laughed. "The stage is a
bit bare at the moment, but we'll
transform it with some curtains and a
proper backdrop. It will look completely
different on the night!"

"There's a lot to do," said Nina seriously. "Will we have time to do it all ourselves?"

Queen Camellia stepped down from her throne and held her wand in the air. "Don't worry about a thing, Nina dear. A fairy queen has many helpers, you know." She waved her wand and called out:

> Gather quickly, fairy helpers.
> This stage must disappear,
> And in its place a market square
> Is what we need right here.
> Petrushka lives in a foreign land
> Where snowy weather reigns,
> So we must cover up this floor,
> These walls and windowpanes.
> I've asked these ballerinas
> To tell us their ideas,
> So gather quickly, helpers,
> Come listen now, my dears!

A host of tiny fairies appeared in a cloud
of rainbow glitter. There were hundreds
of them!

They all curtseyed to the Fairy Queen and their tinkly voices sang out in unison, "Your wish is our command, Your Majesty."

"So it is!" the queen said, smiling. "But today you must pay attention to these three young fairies."

The hall was soon a riot of chattering and laughter as the fairies shared their ideas with the queen and her helpers.

"What we really need is snow," Nina said.

"Yeah, but it can't be real snow or we'll all freeze in our leotards," Bella said.

"And what about an ice rink? That would be so cool!" Peri cried.

"Literally!" Nina laughed.

"Right," said the queen at last. "Helpers – over to you."

The tiny fairies zoomed around the

room, waving their wands and muttering spells. Nina watched them and, just when she thought she would fall down with dizziness, the whirring of wings stopped.

She gasped. It really did seem as though the stage had disappeared! The fairies were now standing in a snowy Russian marketplace. There was a white, wintry backdrop, and snow seemed to be falling gently from the ceiling. There were stalls around the edge of the stage, selling hot drinks, snacks, dolls, music boxes — gifts of every kind imaginable. There was even a merry-go-round, with unicorns rising and falling gently to some soft music.

"Wow!" Bella cried.

"This is going to be a show to remember," Nina whispered.

But then Peri caught sight of the face she recognized from her journey earlier that day. Riding on one of the unicorns

was a cheeky little fairy. The imp
frowned at Peri and put her finger to her
lips as if in warning.

Someone is up to no good, Peri
thought grimly.

Chapter Six

Queen Camellia was very satisfied with the scenery.

"Let's keep it a secret until the show itself," she suggested. She turned to her tiny helpers and dismissed them, then waved her wand. With a shower of petals, the decorations disappeared and the stage returned to normal.

Peri shuffled uncomfortably. I wonder if that fairy on the unicorn can keep a secret, she thought. I must find out who she is.

"Well, I think we've done all we can

in here for the moment, fairies," Queen Camellia said. "Now it's time to talk about the most important part of the show – your costumes!"

Peri perked up at this. "What do you have in mind, Your Majesty?" she asked.

"It's up to you," the queen replied. "Your ideas for the scenery were so good that I'm going to leave you to plan the clothes too. I will lend you my tailor and you can discuss the details with him."

With that, the queen waved her wand and cried:

Juniper Bindweed, come here please –
We need your tailoring expertise!

There was a puff of rose-scented smoke and a skinny fairy appeared. He had a tape measure round his neck and he was coughing and spluttering.

"Your Royal Highness," rasped the fairy, shaking out his wings, "I do wish

you
wouldn't
use that
smokescreen.
It plays havoc
with my hair."

Queen Camellia
raised her eyebrows
and smiled. "I'm sorry,
Juniper. It's just the most
effective way of getting
your attention. I want
you to meet my three
guests, Nina, Peri and
Bella. They are the fairy
ballerinas I told you
about."

"Ah yes, of course!" Juniper beamed
at the trio.

"They have some excellent ideas for
the royal ballet show. I would like you to
listen to them and then go and make the
costumes." Queen Camellia turned to

Nina. "I have other royal business to attend to now, so I'll leave you in Juniper's capable hands. When you've finished, someone will show you to your rooms."

Juniper Bindweed was obviously not used to taking orders from anyone other than the Fairy Queen, but Nina showered him with compliments.

"Honestly, you could charm the wings off a bluebottle!" Bella whispered.

"So tell us, Juniper," Nina continued, ignoring her friend, "you must have so much experience. We are relying on you to help us."

"Yes, well, I have worked here for some time," said Juniper, enjoying the attention. "I made the robes for Her Majesty's coronation, you know. Now, let's have a look at *your* plans, shall we? Why don't you draw me some pictures of the sort of thing you have in mind." He waved his wand and three lily pads and pens appeared.

Nina, Peri and Bella were soon scribbling away, chattering about different fabrics and styles.

"We need so many costumes," Bella explained. "There's even a Dancing Bear in this ballet!"

"Yes, and it's important that our clothes leave us room to move freely," Nina chimed in. "For example, I am planning to do a grand jeté in my dance –"

"What exactly is that?" Juniper asked.

"It's the hardest thing ever – and Nina's brilliant at it!" Peri enthused. "Why don't you show him, Nina?" she suggested.

Nina blushed, but, encouraged by her friends, she agreed. Taking a deep breath, she stood up tall, ran daintily across the room and then leaped gracefully into the air.

"That is amazing!" said Juniper,

clapping his hands. "Your wings didn't move one bit, and yet I could have sworn you were flying."

Nina smiled shyly. "I've been practising lots," she said. "Ever since I fluffed it in my exam."

She glanced sheepishly at Peri.

"Right, I think you should have a knee-length dress, Nina," said Juniper, making some amendments to Nina's designs.

"I have some daisy-chain ballet shoes that I would love to wear – will you be able to match the dress to them, do you think?" Nina asked.

"How charming! Of course, Nina," Juniper said. "Now then, Peri, let's look at the clown outfit. Show me some of the steps you are planning to do."

Peri felt awkward after Nina's stunning performance, but she did as she was told. She stood in second position, her arms held out and got ready to do some spring points. But nothing happened.

"Go on, Peri," said Bella. "What are you waiting for?"

"I – I can't move!" Peri cried. It was true, her feet were glued to the floor.

"Look, we all get nervous from time to time—" Bella started again.

"No, you don't get it!" Peri shouted. "Someone's put a spell on me! I can't move AT ALL!"

And then Peri heard it again – a loud, long, tinkly giggle echoed around the Ballroom.

Chapter Seven

Juniper was very well versed in spell-removal and soon managed to get Peri unstuck.

"Thank you, Juniper," Peri said, stretching out her legs.

Nina and Bella were worried about their friend.

"Do you *really* think someone cast a spell on Peri?" Nina asked. "Who could it have been?"

Juniper shrugged his shoulders. "It was a pretty basic sticking spell. It could have come from somewhere else in the palace by mistake. We are all allowed to use magic to help with our duties, but it has to be said that some of the staff's spells are not quite up to scratch. I wouldn't worry about it. You're all right now, aren't you Peri?"

Peri nodded and gave a weak smile.

"Good," Juniper said. "Well, you've given me a lot of work to do, so I'd better make a start." And he flew off, taking the lily pads and pens with him.

"Listen, guys," said Peri when Juniper was safely out of earshot, "there's something weird going on here. I'm sure someone's watching us."

Nina shook her head. "Don't be silly, Peri. You heard what Juniper said. There's loads of magic floating around inside this place. We're just not used to it because we're not allowed to do spells at the Academy."

"Yeah," Bella agreed. "You're

probably just tired. It's been a long day! Let's go and ask where our rooms are."

Peri reluctantly followed her friends out of the Ballroom.

Over the next few days, Nina and her friends were kept very busy talking to the Fairy Queen and Juniper about the show. They were also involved in planning a party for after the performance, so Peri didn't have time to dwell on the strange things that had happened to her.

Once everything was in place, Queen Camellia arranged for the other fairy ballerinas to come so that they could practise the ballet together.

"When are they coming, Your Majesty?" Nina asked excitedly one morning.

"They should be here any minute now," Queen Camellia replied. "Why don't you three fairies whizz off down to the gates and take a look?"

"Imagine the looks on the others' faces when they see this place!" Bella was saying, her almond eyes sparkling.

"I know. It's the most magical place I've ever seen!" Nina agreed.

"A bit too magical for my liking," Peri muttered.

The three fairy ballerinas arrived at the gates just in time: ten silver dragonfly-drawn carriages, identical to the one the three friends had travelled in, had just landed.

"Where do they keep all those dragonflies?" Nina breathed.

Miss Tremula was there, busily counting the fairy ballerinas out of the coaches and ticking off their names on her clipboard. The fairies looked rather flushed and out of breath.

"Urgh, I don't feel well," complained Nyssa Bean, flying over to Nina. "I've never liked travelling by dragonfly express anyway – but that was something else!"

"It is a bit of a rough ride, isn't it?" Nina said gently. "Don't worry, Nyss, you'll soon forget all about it when you see inside this place."

"Wow!" cried Nyssa's friend Hazel Leafbud, who'd flown over to join her. "There must be, like, ten thousand rooms here!"

"Thirteen thousand actually, modom," a lilac-clad footman chipped in. "Now, kindly follow me. Her Majesty is busy at present, but will come and see you in due course."

Hazel stifled a giggle and Bella raised one eyebrow. "They're all like that! Weird, eh?" she whispered.

The new arrivals were shown to the Ballroom, where Queen Camellia had made some alterations to the stage – there were mirrors on the walls and a barre had been put up along one side.

Miss Tremula quietened her excited pupils and took them through a warm-up to focus their minds and loosen their muscles. Then the real work began.

"Listen carefully, fairies," Miss Tremula said. "Mrs Wisteria has kindly found us a first-rate recording of *Petrushka* on Daisy Disc, so you can hear the music as it should sound with a full orchestra. I understand that Her Majesty will be lending us her own orchestra for the performance. Until then, we shall use this."

Miss Tremula flew over to a Daisy Discplayer and put in the disc.

"Fairies! Please take your places for the market scene!" she called.

Peri and Bella sat down cross-legged to watch. Miss Tremula pressed a button on the discplayer and a jaunty flute sang out. The fairies leaped and twirled around the room, holding out their tutus gracefully. Some of them skipped along with perfectly pointed toes on demi-

pointe, some sprang into pas de chat –
their knees bent, making a neat diamond
shape with their legs.

The ballerinas pirouetted faster and
faster, darting about, using the whole
stage. The music became more agitated
as some brass instruments came in. It
sounds exactly like snow whirling down,
thought Nina.

The string section started up next: violins, violas, cellos — all the instruments were singing out together in a glorious chorus. Nina could see the real marketplace in her mind. There were the stalls, and there was the organ-grinder, piping out music to cheer the frozen crowd.

The whirling and twirling slowed down and Miss Tremula pressed the Stop button. Suddenly the magic of the market faded in Nina's mind and the stage was just an ordinary studio again.

She sighed. "It's *fantastic*!" she cried, clapping her hands.

"Bravo, dears!" cried Miss Tremula. "You are working very hard. Now, we still have to agree on the other solo dances. The one dance I am particularly concerned about is the Dancing Bear—"

But Miss Tremula was cut short by Nina screaming.

"Argh! Fly for your lives!" she yelled,

zooming up to the
ceiling in panic.

A real live bear
was charging
towards her!

Chapter Eight

The bear prowled around the room, leaping up and baring its fangs at the frightened fairies. All the ballerinas had whizzed up to the ceiling to hover next to Nina, and luckily no one had been hurt.

Miss Tremula was trembling even more than usual but, professional as ever, she called out:

Emergency Forces, I summon you!
A dark-magic spell has been cast.
My class is in danger

And under attack.
I beg you to help us — and fast!

WHOOSH! In a flash of green stars a host of palace-guard fairies appeared. They were holding a huge net and they pointed their glinting wands at the bear. Quicker than the beating of a butterfly's wing, they tossed the net over the bear and pinned it down. Then one of the palace guards whistled loudly and the guards and the bear vanished.

The fairy ballerinas were very shaken. Queen Camellia was informed and she immediately ordered that the guests be given hot mugs of chamomile tea.

The Fairy Queen went to speak to Miss Tremula. "Please don't feel you have to continue with the show," she said.

But Miss Tremula was adamant. "The show must go on, Your Majesty," she insisted. "I know you will do all you

can to get to the bottom of this, and in
the meantime we will continue
rehearsing. It does a fairy no good at all
to dwell on disaster."

The queen assured Miss Tremula that
whoever had been responsible for the
dark fairy magic would be severely
punished.

The class spent the rest of the day
practising the whole ballet. Nina went
over her grand jeté again and again.
Bella practised
extravagant demi-
pliés: she bent her
left leg and stretched
out her right, while
holding out one
arm as if to say to
the Ballerina,
"May I have
the pleasure
of this
dance?"

But Peri was feeling more and more
miserable. How can I concentrate when
someone out there wants to ruin the
show? she thought.

More importantly, how could Peri get
her friends to listen to her? She just *knew*
that the fairy on the merry-go-round was
responsible for the bear.

What was Peri going to do?

Nina's class soon forgot about the bear
and enjoyed being pampered at the
palace. Every fairy had been given her
own room and bathroom. The beds were
so soft, Nina said it felt as though she
were sleeping on a cloud!

"You'd better not get too used to
this star treatment," Miss Tremula
joked one morning. "You'll have to
go back to the Academy once the
show is over and you mustn't expect
the same thing there! Now, let's go
from the scene where the Showman

plays his flute and the puppets start to dance."

Nyssa was the Showman. She had a solo dance after the crowd scene at the beginning of the ballet.

"Nina, dear," Miss Tremula said, "at the beginning, the curtains of the puppet theatre will be drawn. When you hear Nyssa's flute dance, you need to get ready. The curtains will then slide back, and you will appear as the Ballerina."

The teacher pressed the Start button on the discplayer; Nyssa performed an artful arabesque and then bent gracefully to pick up an imaginary flute. Silvery sounds floated out of the discplayer.

Nyssa was pirouetting towards Nina now. She swept her right arm back in a graceful arc as if she was drawing a curtain. Nina took the cue and, with her feet in first position and her eyes staring unblinkingly, she looked exactly like a wooden puppet.

Peri watched her
friend closely. She
shuffled closer to
Bella and
whispered, "Isn't
Nina fab? This is
her chance for a
big break, you
know."

"What do you
mean?" Bella
asked.

"Everyone
expects great things
of her because of her
scholarship," Peri
explained. "In the past,
fairies have tried to
sabotage Nina's performances – you
remember I told you what happened to
her before she took her first exam?"

(Poor Nina had ended up in the
Sickbay with a broken leg.)

"But you don't think someone sent the bear to stop Nina dancing?" Bella asked.

"Yes, I do," Peri answered. "And if anyone thinks they're going to ruin things for Nina again, they'll have *me* to reckon with."

Chapter Nine

It was time to try on the costumes. Juniper Bindweed had excelled himself. Nina couldn't believe her eyes.

"Juniper – my dress! It's . . ."

"Gorgeous?" Juniper shrugged. "It's nothing, really."

Nina's dress was a rich, regal purple. It had delicate puffed sleeves and a sweetheart neckline edged with jewels that matched the daisies on her favourite ballet shoes. The tutu was purple gossamer – so light Nina could hardly feel it – and the bodice

was beautifully
fitted.

The other
costumes were just as
magnificent.
Bella had short
trousers and a
tunic made from
colourful fabric which
glimmered and glittered.
She even had a turban!

Peri was equally
amazed. The clown's
outfit was an all-in-one harlequin suit –
a patchwork of colours and
patterns that dazzled and
shone.

Juniper
handed out the
rest of the costumes
to the class.
No one was

disappointed, not even Hazel, who
was to play the part of the Dancing
Bear.

"This is so realistic!" she cried. "It's
not real fur, is it?" she added nervously.

Juniper shot her an offended look. "Of
course not," he said huffily.

When all the fairy ballerinas had their
costumes, Miss Tremula called for
everyone's attention.

"This is our last chance to run
through *Petrushka* before the performance
tomorrow night," she told her pupils.
"Because of this, Her Majesty has put up
some stage curtains and asked the
orchestra to come so that we know
exactly what to expect on the night."

The ballet teacher tapped her wand
on the floor three times. The Ballroom
doors swung open and a fairy orchestra
fluttered in.

Each section was clothed in dazzling
evening wear, but in a different colour,

depending on the instrument. The strings were dressed in green from head to toe; the brass players wore yellow, and the woodwind section was in brilliant blue. All the percussion players looked perfect in purple, but best of all was the conductor, who was covered in sparkling silver sequins. The musicians took their places below the stage, on seats that had been specially arranged for them. Some extra-bright fireflies provided the lighting.

"We will start with the stage curtains drawn and the lights dimmed," Miss Tremula called.

Everyone did as they were told.

The music started quietly, the flute's silvery tones floating up from the orchestra. The fairy ballerinas in the crowd were ready to dart and leap busily around the marketplace, Nyssa was ready to play her flute and Nina was ready to dance.

Rustle! Rustle!

"What's that noise?" Nina called out, stopping the orchestra in mid-flow.

"Nina, dear – concentrate!" said Miss Tremula irritably. "It's probably just a firefly falling. It's quite common to have problems with lighting at rehearsals. I'm so sorry," she said, turning to the conductor, "please, start again."

Rustle! Rustle!

"There it is again, miss!" Nina cried. But this time her warning came too late – CRASH! The curtains collapsed, causing everyone to flutter madly in panic.

In the confusion, Peri heard the unmistakable sound of giggling in a corner of the Ballroom and decided to follow the sound. She zipped out of the room and darted down the corridor. In between the giggles, Peri caught the sound of a few words. I'm getting nearer to the culprit! she thought gleefully.

"Never – without me!" Peri could

hear as she got closer. "That'll – show – not – ignore *me*!"

As Peri rounded the next corner, she caught sight of the fairy mischief-maker. It's the fairy on the unicorn! she thought. I knew it.

"Hey, you!" Peri cried out. "Stop!" The fairy turned and a look of horror crossed her little face. She flew away from Peri at top speed – and came hurtling into the arms of Queen Camellia.

"Coriander?" the queen cried. "What on earth are you doing?"

"That's exactly what I want to know," said Peri grimly.

Princess Coriander tearfully explained to her mother and Peri how fed up she had been ever since the fairy ballerinas had arrived. She was angry that her mother had said she was "too young" to join in.

"You know how much I love ballet,

Mummy!" the little
princess sobbed.
"Why wouldn't you
let me meet the
fairy ballerinas?"

Peri softened.
She reminds me of
Nina's younger sister,
Poppy, she thought.

"It must be hard to
be a fairy princess
and not mix with
normal fairies,"
Peri said kindly.
"Why don't you come
along to the party
after the show? Is that all right, Your
Majesty?" she asked Queen Camellia.

The queen smiled. "Of course. I know
you love ballet, darling," she said to
Coriander. "I was going to let you see
the show – I just thought you'd get bored
watching the rehearsals."

"But you never asked me, Mummy!"
Coriander retorted.

The queen nodded. "You're right,"
she agreed. "I'm sorry. But I really
should punish you for all those tricks
you've been playing on our guests."

Peri butted in quickly. "Don't worry,"
she said. "No harm done. Let's just keep
this between ourselves, shall we?"

Queen Camellia patted Peri on the
shoulder. "All right," she said. "You can
go to the party, Cori. You are lucky that
Periwinkle is such a kind fairy," she said.
"Now we'd better leave Peri to prepare
for tomorrow – it's going to be a big day
for all of us."

Chapter Ten

Show time! Late in the afternoon, dragonfly-drawn carriages arrived from all over fairyland. Queen Camellia had issued a great many invitations. Bella's famous mother, Foxy Glove, had come, and Magnolia Valentine, the prima ballerina who had recommended Nina for the scholarship. But Nina was keen to see her own family. She rushed to greet her mother, Mrs Dewdrop, and her sister, Poppy, and Blossom, her best friend from home. Nina's fairy godmother, Heather

Pimpernel, had also come. Nina was overjoyed to see her.

"I couldn't miss seeing those daisy shoes in action, could I?" Heather said.

Nina introduced her family to Queen Camellia, and in turn the queen brought Princess Coriander to meet the fairy ballerinas.

"I am crazy about ballet – and you're my heroine, Nina!" she gushed.

"It's true, Nina," said the Fairy Queen. "Coriander has heard so much about you. In fact, I have a special request . . ."

"Of course, Your Majesty," said Nina excitedly.

"Coriander is so keen to learn ballet, and I was wondering if you would like to come and live here at the palace and be her personal tutor?" the Fairy Queen asked.

"Oh, er, well . . ." Nina faltered, looking nervously at her family and friends. "That is a wonderful offer . . ."

Queen Camellia smiled. "I know it's a big thing to ask. Have a think about it, Nina, and come and find me after the show." And the Fairy Queen took her daughter by the hand and flew off.

Nina turned to her friends. "What should I do?" she asked them anxiously.

"You should stay," Peri said, desperately trying not to cry.

"Yeah, Peri's right," said Bella. "It's too good an offer to turn down." And she looked at the floor and fiddled nervously with her hairclips.

Nina was bewildered. I don't think they would miss me at all, she thought sadly.

It was time for the performance. The orchestra started tuning up and the audience took their seats. The Ballroom chandelier was sparkling brightly. Everything was perfect. Finally, Queen Camellia and Princess Coriander took their seats in the front row.

The curtains rolled softly back and the audience gasped with delight. All the decorations were exactly as Nina and her friends had requested – the magical snow was falling gently from the ceiling, the stalls were full of wonderful gifts and mouthwatering food, and the ballerinas' costumes dazzled.

As the trumpets blasted out a joyful
tune, a fairy ballerina cavorted across the
stage in a raucous Russian Cossack dance.
She alternated between grand pliés and
grand battements, squatting down low and
then leaping up high, kicking her legs out
to the side. The crowd milled around,
pirouetting, skipping and jumping on
spring points. And the Dancing Bear
leaped and twirled in the background.

Nyssa was so captivating as the cruel
Showman that the audience began
hissing and booing! Peri was very
convincing as Petrushka the clown. As
the woodwind instruments played their
jaunty little tune, she flopped her head
from side to side and skipped from one
foot to the other in a jerky dance. Bella
was wonderful as the handsome Moor,
dancing mockingly in front of Petrushka.

Well done, Peri and Bella, Nina
thought to herself. That's the best you've
ever danced!

The ballet progressed smoothly, telling the story of poor Petrushka who loved the Ballerina with all his heart, but knew he didn't have a chance next to the handsome Moor. The audience was completely caught up in the magical tale.

Now for the hardest bit, thought Nina.

Nina got ready to do her grand jeté.

She took a deep breath, ran daintily across the stage holding out her tutu – and, opening out her arms, she jumped! She floated through the air, and the audience stared open-mouthed at this graceful ballerina, flying without a flutter of her fairy wings.

I've done it! Nina thought, as she landed soundlessly in first position.

The ballet ended in a flurry of strings. The audience leaped to its feet, clapping and cheering. One by one, the fairy ballerinas took centre stage and curtseyed. And when Nina took her place, the audience showered her with rose petals and sequins.

"Well done, Nina!" Peri shouted above the applause. "You're practically a prima ballerina now!"

After the show the fairy ballerinas rushed off to the party. There were tables groaning with the fairies' favourite food.

Nina's sister, Poppy, couldn't believe her eyes.

"Don't drink too much of the sparkling elderflower, Poppy dear," said Mrs Dewdrop. "I don't want you burping in front of the queen. Ah, Nina! There you are – what a wonderful show—" She stopped, seeing that Nina was crying. "Whatever is the matter?"

"I don't know whether or not to take Queen Camellia up on her offer," Nina sobbed. "And I'm worried my friends don't care one way or the other!"

Her mother comforted her. "Nina darling – your friends only want what's best for you. Of course they'd miss you, but they are trying not to think of themselves," she said.

"Do you think so?" Nina sniffed.

"You know Mum's right," said Poppy. "She *always* is," she added, rolling her eyes.

"What shall I do, Mum?" asked Nina.

"Follow your heart, dear," Mrs Dewdrop advised.

Nina nodded and went to find Queen Camellia who was chatting to Peri and Bella.

"Ah, Nina – have you made up your mind?" the queen asked. "Your friends here seem to think you will make the right decision."

"Yes," Nina said quietly. "I'm afraid, Your Majesty, that I do not want to leave the Academy – or my friends – quite yet." She looked at the queen nervously.

"That's all right," Queen Camellia said, patting her on the arm. "I can see

your friends are more important to you
than fame or fortune. That is why you
would be such a good role model for
Coriander. Perhaps she can come and
stay with you at the Academy one day.
Here," the Fairy Queen added.
"Coriander asked me to give you this."
She smiled and handed Nina a tiara
gleaming with glittering gems. "You
deserve it, Nina."

Peri and Bella threw their arms
around their friend, tears streaming down
their faces. "We're *so* glad you're staying
with us!" they cried.

"How could I
leave you two?"
Nina said, laughing
and hugging her
friends. "After all,
as Madame Dupré
said, no one's
going to split up the
Dream Team!"

Collect three tokens and get this gorgeous Nina Fairy Ballerina ballet bag!

There's a token at the back of each Nina Fairy Ballerina book - collect three tokens, and you can get your very own, totally FREE Nina Fairy Ballerina ballet bag.

Send your three tokens, along with your name, address and parent/guardian's signature
(you must get your parent/guardian's permission to take part in this offer)
to: Nina Fairy Ballerina Ballet Bag Offer, Marketing Department, Macmillan Children's Books, 20 New Wharf Road, London N1 9RR

Nina Fairy Ballerina Bag Offer

1 Token

Collect 3 tokens and get your free ballet bag!
Valid until 31/12/06

A selected list of titles available from Macmillan Children's Books

The prices shown below are correct at the time of going to press. However, Macmillan Publishers reserves the right to show new retail prices on covers which may differ from those previously advertised.

Anna Wilson

Nina Fairy Ballerina New Girl	0 330 43985 5	£3.99
Nina Fairy Ballerina Daisy Shoes	0 330 43986 3	£3.99
Nina Fairy Ballerina Best Friends	0 330 43987 1	£3.99
Nina Fairy Ballerina Show Time	0 330 43988 X	£3.99

All Pan Macmillan titles can be ordered from our website, www.panmacmillan.com, or from your local bookshop and are also available by post from:

Bookpost, PO Box 29, Douglas, Isle of Man IM99 1BQ
Credit cards accepted. For details:
Telephone: 01624 677237
Fax: 01624 670923
Email: bookshop@enterprise.net
www.bookpost.co.uk

Free postage and packing in the United Kingdom